Dear Sam and
Beth —
Have fun with Panchos
Love Alex xx.

Alexandra spent her early years in Pakistan and Africa before coming to live in England. *Pandemonium in New York* came out of a trip to America, where she lost her panda in the Empire State Building which was sent back to England with a note of his travels. Alexandra worked for 40 years in the NHS, mostly in Children and Young Peoples Services. Alexandra lives with her husband, Tim, in Oxfordshire. She has 3 grown-up children and 5 grandchildren who are her pride and joy.

Pandemonium in New York

Alexandra Hammond

AUSTIN MACAULEY PUBLISHERS™

LONDON • CAMBRIDGE • NEW YORK • SHARJAH

Copyright © Alexandra Hammond (2019)

A CIP catalogue record for this title is available from the British Library.

ISBN 9781788786720 (Paperback)
ISBN 9781788786737 (Hardback)
ISBN 9781788786744 (E-Book)
www.austinmacauley.com

First Published (2019)
Austin Macauley Publishers Ltd
25 Canada Square
Canary Wharf
London
E14 5LQ

My grandchildren: Rebekah, Anna, Eliza,
Hettie and Otto, and any others that may come along!

To my husband, Tim, who believed in this book. My father, Ronald Sayers, who came up with the title. To the children who helped me with feedback and told me what was funny and believable – in particular, Rebekah and Anna Meathrel, Eliza Hammond and Ben Lever. To my family and friends, many of whom are teachers, who encouraged me to put the story in print.

Chapter 1

"Ouch!" cried Ponchos, rubbing his sore head, "where on earth am I?" A great big lump was appearing on his head behind his left ear. Everything looked blurred and upside down, and then he realised he was upside down so he slowly righted himself, groaning until he was sitting on a step the right way up.

Ponchos shook his head and rubbed his ears which he was inclined to do when he was muddled. Then he remembered how he had fallen. He was sitting in a rucksack on Rebekah's back, coming down the stairs of a large building in New York. The Empire State Building in America. Someone had caught his attention; it was a very tall, thin man, almost bony with a black moustache that looked like a wet slimy slug sitting in front of his nose. He was wearing a black felt hat with a badge that had a snake on it which Ponchos thought was very creepy.

He was whispering behind his bony hand to a short round man with a very large bottom that was dressed in striped and star trousers which, Ponchos thought, looked very busy and American. What had caught Ponchos' attention was hearing the words, "Panda", "Zoo", "Kidnap".

Ponchos was a very rare, unusual sort of a panda not found at zoos but made in factories in places like China. He was given to Rebekah on her

7th birthday from her Great Grandpa Ronald Stanley, who had travelled all over the world. Rebekah and her sisters, Anna, Eliza and Hettie loved Ponchos very much.

Ponchos had wanted to get a closer look and be able to hear a little better so he leaned closer to the men and lost his balance. The next thing he remembered was lying upside down on the steps.

Ponchos looked around and there was no sign of the family, in fact, there was no sign of anyone at all. It was very dark and eerie, and very quiet. Ponchos sat with his head in his hands; he knew he was in big trouble, alone in New York. A big tear rolled down his black and white face, and then splashed on the step making a little puddle. He looked at the clock, it was late. He felt frightened and alone.

Ponchos had never been left on his own before; he had always been with one of his family. He was a favourite with all of the girls because he was such a fabulous friend. If you felt sad, he would give you a bear hug wrapping his paws around you very tightly. He would make you laugh by pulling funny faces and sticking his bottom in the air. If you felt angry, you could go to Ponchos and shout as loudly as you like, and he would just listen and suggest you went out and kicked a ball or jumped up and down. If you felt happy, he would be happy with you singing your favourite songs. If you felt worried, he would just sit with you and say, "Now, what's the worst that could happen?"

Ponchos knew that his family would be as worried as he was. They would be wondering what on earth had happened to him.

Ponchos had been so excited visiting the Empire State Building. It was the last trip the family were making before flying home to England. The tour of the Building had been so interesting, the tour guide so entertaining. He was called Mr Shorts Jigger, who certainly lived up to his name; he never kept still, jigging up and down as he spoke, waving his arms, shouting and getting so excited that sweat ran down his face, making his moustache all wet and soggy and even more slug like.

"It used to be the tallest building in the world, you see," he said jumping up and down, "it has a lightning rod near the top of the building, and it gets struck by lightning at least 3 times a year, you see," he said, shrieking and twisting his body in funny crazy shapes, making a hissing noise. "Sometimes when couples kiss, they get an electric shock." Ponchos giggled as he imagined leaning in to give a great big smoochy kiss to his friend Tyger and then both leaping in the air, hair and ears all standing on end.

As Ponchos was thinking about the tour, trying to cheer himself up, something very clear came into his head. Why, the man whispering to the short round man on the stairs was the tour guide, Mr Shorts Jigger. It was the snake on the hat that triggered his memory as Mr Shorts Jigger reminded Ponchos of a slippery slimy snake.

Ponchos slowly picked himself up, climbed down the stairs and hummed his favourite song, "When you're feeling all alone, and your pants are full of foam, diarrhoea, diarrhoea," which he always did to help him feel brave. He decided that he would try and find out a bit more about Mr Shorts Jigger and visit Central Park Zoo, and then try and find his lovely family, Rebekah, Anna, Eliza and Hettie in time to go back to England.

The doors and windows were all locked, and there was nothing else to do but to break the box of glass that said fire alarm and then wait for some action. As Ponchos expected, the alarm went off immediately; the noise was deafening, with his fingers in his ears, he hid behind a table shaking as the fire doors slammed shut.

Chapter 2

You have never seen such a sight. There was a crash like thunder and bright lights flashing like lightning as about fifty fire workers rushed in with their hoses and helmets, charging up the stairs shouting, "Where is the fire?"

Ponchos did feel very bad as he watched the fire workers all rushing around trying to find the fire. He had been taught the dangers of raising false alarms, and how it could stop fire workers attending a real fire, but he felt it was his only way out of the building. Ponchos slipped out quietly into the night on an adventure that he had no idea where it would take him.

He was now feeling extremely hungry; he could hear the rumbling of his tummy. One thing about Ponchos was that no matter how sad or frightened he was, he always wanted to eat. He was drawn to a bright light with a sign that said "Wendy's". He followed his nose, the smell of the burgers and fries drawing him in.

"Hi, little feller, what can I get you?" said a young lady with pink hair. Ponchos thought this must be Wendy. She certainly didn't look like any Wendy he had known in England. All the Wendys he had met were cuddly and smelt of lavender.

"Hello, Wendy, can you get me a milkshake, burger and fries?" he said as confidently as possible, knowing full well he had no money to pay for the food.

Ponchos put on his saddest and cutest face which he often used when he was in any kind of trouble. "Are you alone?" said the pink haired lady, "You look very young to be out at this time of night."

Ponchos thought very carefully before he replied. "Not exactly," desperately trying to think of a good excuse, but fortunately at that moment, the pink haired lady got interrupted by a flood of new customers. Ponchos smiled and pointed to a very large family, hoping that the waitress would think they were his family. They were a big family and very loud. The dad was tall with a grumpy face, the mum looked tired which wasn't surprising as they seemed to have a lot of children. Ponchos counted about seven children all at different ages and stages dressed in all different styles. They all seemed to talk at once and ordered lots of food and milk shakes. Ponchos was glad that they were not like his real family.

Ponchos slipped of his stool and mingled amongst the children who were so busy arguing with each other that they didn't notice a little furry black paw reach up and take a burger and milk shake of the counter, and silently walk out.

He heard the dad shout,
"Hey we are one short of a burger and milk shake."
The pink haired lady replied, "What about the little black and white feller that was with you, perhaps he has it."

The man roared as he saw Ponchos leg it down fifth Avenue. "Oy, you furry Brit, come back with my burger, you little ruffian."

"Oh dear," Ponchos said, "I hardly know myself! First setting off the alarm and now stealing food of an American, whatever next." The burger tasted delicious, lots of onions and cheese with a big dollop of tomato sauce; the milkshake was strawberry, and Ponchos gave a contented sigh after everything was finished, leaving him with a red moustache.

It was very dark by the time Ponchos arrived at the zoo; it was all shut up, and the gates were closed. He could hear eerie animal sounds: a roar of a lion, a monkey screeching, and the trumping of an elephant, but how was he going to get in?

Ponchos sat down and tried not to panic. He had never been out alone at night and especially in a strange country where everything was different. He tried to breathe more slowly and deeply to calm himself down in order to think.

The only clue he had was the words "Panda" and "zoo" being whispered by Mr Shorts Jigger to the round man with a stripey bottom.

He slowly walked around the entrance and found a notice on a gate which read, "Come and see the new baby Panda, on loan from China. Mother and baby doing well. Only here for two more weeks."

Whilst he was thinking, he picked up a leaflet from the ground. It was all about the zoo and what's more, it had a map of where all the animals were. There was a children's part which had a large whale statue at the entrance, called "Whaley". "Not a very original name," Ponchos thought, "you would expect them to come up with a better one than that." He looked for where the Pandas lived on the map and then yawned loudly. He suddenly felt very tired, and the next minute he had closed his eyes and fell into a deep sleep, leaning against the entrance gate with this leg sticking out between the bars and began to snore loudly.

Ponchos was in a very dangerous position. Unbeknown to him, Mr Shorts Jigger and his little fat friend were walking towards the entrance gate talking softly and laughing, as they were planning to steal the baby panda and make a lot of money.

Would they see Ponchos? What could they do to him? They were capable of anything.

Chapter 3

Ponchos woke with a start as he felt something squash his leg, and it hurt like mad. He tried not to scream when he realised it was Mr Shorts Jigger standing on his leg! "Idiot!" he muttered to himself. He bit his lip to stop himself from calling out, thankful it hadn't been the fat one which would have made his leg hurt more. Mercifully, they hadn't seen him in the dark night. Ponchos held his breath until the two men moved through the gate. Ponchos followed very close behind through the now opened gate, being very careful that they didn't see or hear him. Ponchos now realised that these men were not nice at all. He didn't like the way they talked, the way they walked and the sly way they laughed. They were nasty. Really nasty.

Mr Shorts Jigger and his friend who was called Trumps sat down near the lion's enclosure. Trumps got out a pipe and began to blow smoke which made Ponchos want to cough. He crept nearer to the men lying flat on his tummy and hid behind a tree. He could now hear the men talking.

Trumps, it was clear, worked at the zoo and had a key. He knew the zoo back to front. He had made himself become a very trusted friend to all the animals and other zoo keepers who loved him. He was funny and silly and made them laugh. What they didn't know was that Trumps was mean and worked with Mr Shorts Jigger who was a thief in disguise. He stole rare

animals and sold them on at a great price. Trumps was his accomplice. They had been so successful because Trumps had worked at lots of zoos, and no one had ever suspected him of being a very wicked and devious man. Children particularly liked him as he would tell funny jokes and pretend to be interested in their hobbies. Mr Shorts Jigger was not liked because he was as sly as a snake and mean looking and sniffed a lot. Bogeys would often be seen just under his nose, and he never used a hanky. People would laugh at him behind his back because he was odd. They didn't suspect that he too was greedy for money and would do anything to get it. Why, he had even sold his own animals, including a beautiful ginger fluffy cat and a bunny with stand-up ears.

Trumps and Mr Shorts Jigger were discussing a plan to steal the baby panda; they were going to hold the baby as ransom and get the Americans to pay. "They will pay a lot," said Trumps, "they will be so embarrassed that the baby panda has been stolen as he is on loan from China." They rubbed their hands in glee thinking of the money they would get, and how they would spend it. They laughed that dirty dark laugh as they thought how they would spend the money. "It's as easy as taking a baby away from its mother." Mr Shorts Jigger laughed.

Ponchos was horrified; he couldn't believe his ears. What vile person would steal a baby from his mother? Ponchos knew what it felt like to be parted from his family. It was a terrible feeling of sadness and fear. It felt like a big knot was in your tummy, and you couldn't breathe properly. He could imagine what the baby and the mother would feel like being parted from each other.

Here he was in the middle of New York by the Central Zoo, all alone with no detective experience and hearing of a major kidnap that would not only affect the baby and its poor mother, but embarrass the American people and the president of the United States. What was he to do? Who would believe a little chap who had already set off a fire alarm and stolen food? He may even have been caught on CCTV. He wasn't even a very brave panda, he didn't really like adventures. He liked reading about them, but it was very different actually being in one. He was missing his home where life was easier and a lot more comfortable. He thought that he would never complain of being bored which he sometimes did at home when he couldn't think of anything to do. Right now, he wished he was bored and everything was the same.

Ponchos started humming again, "When you're far away from home, and your pants are full of foam, diarrhoea, diarrhoea." Ponchos was a very kind panda; he couldn't bear the thought of the baby being taken by these cruel men, so he decided he would have to be brave and try and think of how he was going to save the panda.

Mr Shorts Jigger and Trumps were going to come back the following night to steal the baby. They were going to give the mother panda some pills to make her very sleepy. Trumps was going to put them in her supper. When she would be deeply asleep, Trumps would go in and take the baby panda, wrap him in a blanket and take him to a waiting car that would be driven by Mr Shorts Jigger. The car would then take the panda to a secret location until the ransom money was paid.

"Easy," laughed Trumps. Both men then walked confidently out of the gate and down the road; all Ponchos could see was smoke circles coming from Trumps' pipe billowing up into the night's sky.

"We will see about that," said Ponchos, "we will wipe the smile off your smug faces." Then he realised that there wasn't a "we" only an "I".

Chapter 4

Ponchos needed to think very fast; he had only a short time to save the panda.

He decided to make his way to the panda enclosure to see if he could make contact with the mother panda. "I wonder if she speaks any English, she may only speak Chinese." Ponchos did not know any Chinese so that could be a big problem. He arrived at the enclosure and saw the mother panda asleep with the most gorgeous black and white fluffy baby panda he had ever seen. Ponchos immediately fell in love with him. He couldn't stop staring at this most beautiful creature.

"Excuse me," Ponchos whispered not wanting to startle the mother, "do you speak English?" The mother panda opened one eye and then jumped, nearly dropping the sleeping baby. "Excuse me," persisted Ponchos, "do you speak English?"

The mother panda looked with disbelief. "Who and what are you?" Ponchos pushed out his chest and introduced himself. "My name is Ponchos, and I am a panda like you. Only, I was made in a factory in China. I may look a little odd but I am very clever." Ponchos remembered he hadn't the time to be offended. "Look," said Ponchos, "I have come to warn you that there is a plan afoot to steal your baby tomorrow; men are going to

23

demand money to release him. I heard the men talking tonight. One of the men is called Trumps who works at the zoo. They are going to put sleeping pills in your supper tomorrow night and then when you are deeply asleep, they are going to steal your baby."

"Ha ha ha, very funny, best joke I've heard all year," the mother panda said. "Trumps is the most popular keeper in the Zoo; everyone likes him. He gives me extra treats and spoils the baby. You must have misunderstood; why, you are only a scraggy sort of a fellow, why would I trust you? Go away, you will frighten my baby if he wakes up and sees you."

Ponchos felt desperate. How was he going to make this mother understand that her baby was going to be kidnapped? That she may never see him again. Ponchos decided to walk away and think how he was going to convince the mother.

Ponchos sat down near the elephant enclosure and sighed very loudly. He felt something wet on his cheek; he looked up and saw an enormous grey trunk kissing his cheek. He jumped up with his heart beating very fast.

"Hi, panda, are you OK?" said the Elephant.

"No," said Ponchos, "I am not OK. I am upset and lonely. I feel very hot and flustered; I am having a terrible time, and I haven't a clue what to do."

"Tell me your problems," the Elephant said in a very soothing voice, "I am very good at listening. Tell Solomon what's troubling you. I am called Solomon after a very wise King in the Bible. He was so wise that many people sought his advice, even the Queen of Sheba."

For the first time since the fall, Ponchos thought he could trust this kindly elephant, so he sat down and tucked himself under the elephant's trunk and told him the whole story from the beginning to the end. He talked about his family and big tears fell down his cheek as he wondered if he would ever see them again. Solomon just listened and made soothing noises and hugged Ponchos through the fence with his trunk. When Ponchos came to the end, he just sat and looked sadly at Solomon and waited for Solomon to speak.

It seemed like a very long time before Solomon spoke but when he did, it was so gentle and kind that Ponchos felt he had made a friend for life. One of those rare times when you meet someone who you know is good and kind and is going to help you get out of a very tight spot.

Solomon said, "Ponchos, I believe you. I know you are telling the truth, and I will help you."

Ponchos felt such relief, he was believed and this wonderful elephant was going to help him; he was no longer alone.

Chapter 5

Ponchos then fell asleep, feeling very warm and safe for the first time since he had fallen out of the ruck sack. He dreamt of Rebekah, Anna, Eliza and Hettie, of being back at home in England, picking strawberries in the garden and playing hide and seek. A big smile spread over his fluffy face. Solomon let him sleep for a few hours as he could see how very tired and weary this funny little furry creature was. Whilst he slept, Solomon did some thinking. Whilst thinking, Solomon made funny little noises, a few sighs and blew a few breaths as he tried to work out a plan.

Solomon gently woke Ponchos who took a few minutes to realise where he was and that he wasn't at home, and this wasn't all a dream. The picture of his family faded. He sat up and looked at Solomon with sad and questioning eyes. "What do we do? Can we save the baby panda?"

Solomon took a while to answer, "Yes, I believe we have to try; we have to get some other animals on board to help. We don't have a lot of time; its early in the morning and in the early hours of tomorrow morning the baby will be kidnapped so we have to work fast." Ponchos nodded his head and put aside his longing to go home.

Solomon called out to Ponchos to follow, "First, we will talk to Lenny the lion as Trumps is his keeper, we have to find a way of making him believe us."

The lion enclosure was next to the elephant house; Ponchos slipped through the fence and walked closely to Solomon.

Lenny was a very lazy and snooty lion. He really did think he was the very best and cleverest animal in the zoo. He was rather fat because he did a lot of eating and sleeping. It didn't help one little bit that he was spoilt by all the keepers, particularly, Trumps who gave him lots of sugary snacks which lions really shouldn't eat. Lenny didn't really have many friends amongst the animals because he just couldn't be bothered to be nice to them. He often growled and said unkind words. The only animal, Lenny had any time for, was Solomon because he realised that Solomon was kind and also rather large.

"Hi, Lenny," called Solomon. "We need to have a talk with you; we have a problem. Can you spare us a minute?" Lenny sleepily walked over, not very happy that his sleep was being disturbed. Ponchos had never been in the same side of a cage as a lion and felt very nervous. He slipped out from behind Solomon and shyly said hello. Stuttering, he told the story of the plan to kidnap the baby panda. Lenny looked amused and then looked at Solomon who just nodded and then told Ponchos to continue.

"You can't be serious," said Lenny, "Trumpy is my keeper and does everything I want him to; why would he want to steal a panda? I am the only animal worth stealing at this zoo, not a smelly panda."

There was something about Ponchos and his story that made Lenny wonder if it was true. He had often heard Trumps boasting on the telephone about making a lot of money and something about a baby but Lenny didn't care because Trumps always gave him treats and spoiled him.

Lenny paced up and down trying to think, which was hard for him because he didn't think very often. He did think it might be quite fun to be involved in a plan to stop a kidnap. It might even make him famous! He didn't really care about the panda.

He said to Solomon and Ponchos, "OK guys, what do we do next?" Solomon said, "Lenny, when Trumps comes in this morning which won't be long, you have got to get his keys; the keys open all the cages of the zoo. When you get the keys, give them to me, and I will give them to Ponchos. Ponchos you then open all the cages, and once you have done that, return the keys to me and then, Lenny, you take the keys back to Trumps before he knows they are gone."

"Now," Solomon continued, "we have to let all the animals know what is happening; Lenny, you tell Sidney, the chief monkey, what is happening and tell him to shout it out to all the animals; he has a voice like a foghorn. Tell them all the gates of the cages will be unlocked; they are not to attempt to get out until they get instructions from Solomon. Be quick, we only have an hour to get the word out before Trumps comes in. Ponchos, you go back to the Panda house and you have to find a way of making Chichi, the mother panda, believe you."

Ponchos ran to the panda house and on the way, he could hear the loudest screeching from the monkey house; it must be Sidney, he couldn't understand what he was saying as it was in a very strong American accent, but he could make out some words like "emergency", "creep for real".

Ponchos knew he had to make the mother panda believe him; otherwise, all would be lost. The baby would be taken and possibly never be seen again.

Chapter 6

Ponchos was out of breath when he arrived; he could hardly speak. He knew Sidney had done his work as the mother Panda rushed to the edge of the enclosure. "I am so sorry I didn't believe you." sobbed the mother. "Please help us, please don't let them steal my baby. He will be so frightened; he has never left my side, not even for a moment."

Ponchos took her paws in his and looked into her frightened eyes and said, "I am going to do everything I can to stop the kidnap but you have to help us. You have to pretend to act normally and not give the game away." Ponchos slowly went through the plan, making sure Chichi, the mother, understood every part of it. Part of the plan was that Ponchos would pretend he was the baby panda. He would lie next to the mother under the blanket. When Trumps and Mr Shorts Jigger would come to steal the baby, they would think in the dark that Ponchos was the real baby panda. Meanwhile, the baby would be safely tucked away safe and sound.

Ponchos ran back to Solomon, relieved that Chichi had believed him and would work with them.

"Well done, Ponchos." said Solomon. "So far, the animals are with us; they are actually quite excited; we haven't had an adventure like this before."

Before Solomon stopped speaking, they could hear a whistling noise,

and there was Trumps striding towards the lion enclosure. "Hello, Kitty," purred Trumps, "How's my favourite pussy cat?" Lenny rubbed his head against Trumps knees and swiftly took the keys out of his back pocket with his mouth and slowly walked towards the elephant enclosure. Trumps was too busy on his phone to notice, chortling to whoever was on the other phone. "Looking forward to that beach and all that sunshine." he joked. The good thing about Trumps was that he was always on the phone and so missed most of what was going on in life. Lenny was surprised that he didn't have a crooked neck as he held the phone between his head and shoulder. Lenny wondered if it was a good thing being on the phone all the time. Trumps was unaware that his keys had been stolen!

Lenny gave the keys to Solomon who quickly gave them to Ponchos. "Now be quick, open all the gates and bring those keys back before Trumps knows they are missing."

Ponchos ran as fast as his little legs could go. He opened all the animal cages, urging the animals to wait and stay put until they were given their orders.

Out of breath, he handed the keys to Solomon who walked slowly over to Lenny. Lenny picked them up in his mouth and slipped them quietly back into Trumps back pocket, nuzzling Trumps back so he wouldn't notice. Trumps ruffled Lenny's neck and walked out locking the Lion enclosure. Everyone breathed a sigh of relief.

Lenny looked pleased with himself and then gave a very loud roar that made Ponchos and Solomon jump. "Oh no," Lenny wailed in disbelief, "I can't get out. Trumps has locked my cage. You wallies! You idiots!" he roared with anger and frustration.

Solomon and Ponchos hadn't thought that Trumps would of course lock the lion enclosure when he went out. However, all the other gates were open, and they knew that the other keepers would not go in to the enclosure now as all the animals had been fed and cleaned.

"Oh, Lenny we are so sorry, you can still help us with our plan to save the baby."

Lenny was not happy. "Without me, you are doomed! You can't keep the animals under control; you have a hopeless team." Solomon and Ponchos were inclined to agree but said nothing.

They sat there looking blank and worried. All the gates of the animals were open; there was potential for great disaster; the animals were waiting for the next instruction. If they didn't get one, they just might take matters in their own hands and riot, and there would be pandemonium,not just in the zoo but all over New York.

Among all the animals, there were the elephants: Solomon and his wife Hattie. They were the wisest of the animals. Monkeys: Riley and Sidney who were both very unpredictable and noisy. Penguins: Charlie, Gracie and Ruby. Gracie was the most adventurous of the penguins, whilst Ruby was shy, and Charlie was just very funny and made everybody laugh. There was an enormous gorilla, who was not very clever, called Pater Cake. Last of all, there was a polar bear called Bev who was quiet and could be trusted to do whatever she was told.

As they sat there looking worried, they could hear rumbles of impatience coming from the animals. "What's the plan, big boy?" Sidney called out to Solomon, "We want to know; we are getting worried, who's in charge of this plan?" Sidney was agitated, red faced and pacing up and down making everyone feel very nervous. Ponchos and Solomon realised they didn't have an ideal group to work with, but it was all they had, and they were going to have to do their very best to save the baby.

So, Ponchos took a very deep breath. He knew he had to take control of the situation. It was now or never. With all the courage, he could muster, he stood up threw out his chest and in the loudest voice he could manage, he shouted, "Animals of Central Zoo New York, are you with me? We have to stop the kidnap of the baby panda; we have to stop these criminals from taking rare and beautiful animals and selling them to make money. You could be next! We must be brave and strong and work together to save America. This is the plan as follows."

Chapter 7

It was becoming very dark, and there was a sound of silence; you could feel the tension in the air. It felt spooky. It felt scary. The animals were all in place ready to take on Trumps and Mr Shorts Jigger. They were all very nervous, knowing that the life of the baby panda depended on them.

The penguins were all by the gate, hiding behind the fences. Charlie was trying not to giggle with nerves. Pater Cake was just inside the panda enclosure hiding her great bulk behind the panda house, going over in her head what she had to do.

Sidney and Riley were up some trees on the path leading to the Panda house, hiding in the branches. Sidney was biting his nails which he did when he was nervous. Bev, the polar bear, was sitting quietly by the exit. Her role was not to let anyone out.

Ponchos lay down quietly by the mother panda, pretending to be the baby panda, the blanket over him. Both Chichi's and Ponchos' hearts were beating very fast and loudly. The baby panda, unaware of all the excitement had been safely tucked away in the elephant house all warm and cosy.

Suddenly, there was the sound of a very soft whistle; in the darkness, the penguins could just about make out the shadow of the two men, one tall and thin the other small and fat.

Mr Shorts Jigger looked nervous as he and Trumps walked to the gate. As they entered the gate, one of the penguins who couldn't be seen spat on his shoe and bit his foot. "Ouch, you Wally burger! You've trodden on my foot." he shouted at Trumps and cuffed him around the ear.

"No, I didn't, you clumsy idiot, you must have tripped." spat Trumps. On and on, they went down the path to the Panda house. Suddenly, Trumps felt something very wet running down his back, bottom and his legs. "Yuk, something wet has gone all over my trousers." Sidney was doubled up with laughter his hand over his mouth so he didn't cry out and give the game away. Sidney had done a wee bang on Trumps back from the tree up ahead.

"Trumps you've wet yourself." Mr Shorts Jigger shouted. "Couldn't you have waited?"

"I have not," Trumps said crossly, "It must have been a bird."

"Massive bird then," said Mr Shorts Jigger, "I have never seen such a big wee."

They both began to feel a bit nervous. "Something is not right." Trumps said, "There is a mystery in the air. I can't put my finger on it." On they went, looking around them, eyes wide and hair standing on end. They reached the panda enclosure and went in. They could just make out the mother panda and a shape that looked like the baby lying closely next to her.

At that moment, Pater Cake the Gorilla came forward; her great looming body came face to face with Trumps and Mr Shorts Jigger.

"Goodness gracious mercy me!" Trumps yelled.

"Agh, oh yikes!" cried Mr Shorts Jigger as Pater Cake sat down on his head. Pater Cake was so excited she passed wind from her enormous bottom right onto Mr Shorts Jigger's face. The smell was deadly, a terrible mix of overcooked sprouts, manure and rotten fish. Mr Shorts Jigger could hardly breathe. Pater Cake had a great, big smile all over her face as she made herself comfortable. All you could see was Mr Shorts Jigger's ears on either side of Pater Cake's bottom!

It was all going so well; everyone had performed to the plan. Exactly right and then, everything went very wrong.

Sidney, who was always going to be the weak link in the chain, decided he wanted a bigger role. Instead of waiting in the tree as instructed, he gave the wrong command to all the animals. "It's Commander Sidney speaking; I am taking over from Solomon; we need to march as an army with roaring sounds to the exit. As Mr Shorts Jigger and Trumps run to the exit, we will attack them. On the count of 10, we will go."

Before Solomon could even think what was happening on the count of Sidney's 10, the animals all roared and headed off to the exit, not knowing that this was not part of the plan. The sound was terrible like thunder and lightning, and guns, and screaming of every type of beast you could imagine. Pater Cake who wasn't the brightest of gorillas got up and headed for the exit, forgetting that she was letting go of the enemy.

As quick as lightning, Trumps and Mr Shorts Jigger leapt up, threw a blanket over what they thought was the baby panda and ran in the opposite direction to the animals towards the entrance. They got straight into the getaway car that was waiting for them, and the car sped off into the night.

Chapter 8

Solomon was so angry when he got to the exit and watched all the animals go through the gate. He could hardly speak; he was so furious. "You fools, I told you to listen only to me for instructions. Sidney gave the wrong command. The men have now escaped by running to the entrance and have taken Ponchos with them, thinking he was the baby panda."

The animals were horrified. Sidney looked stone faced. "What do you have to say for yourself, Sidney?" Solomon shouted. Sidney said nothing. What he had done began to sink in. He wasn't a bad monkey, just silly and selfish, and he hadn't realised what his actions would lead to. He only wanted to feel important and be the boss. That one moment of power had now resulted in a terrible consequence. He felt sick. He didn't know what to say.

"We will have to try and find Ponchos." Solomon said. All the animals apart from Lenny who could be heard muttering, "Idiots, I knew it would go wrong without me," walked slowly through the gate into the street along Fifth Avenue, a place where they had never gone before.

Meanwhile Ponchos was covered in a smelly blanket on the back seat of a car that was moving very fast. He was lying between Mr Shorts Jigger and Trumps.

Ponchos was very frightened; his paws were very sweaty, and his heart was going very fast; he could hardly breathe. To calm himself, he thought of his lovely family, and big tears ran down his face. Would he ever see them again?

He knew he was in a very big fix. He was trying to remember what had gone wrong. Sidney had shouted something; he couldn't quite hear what under the blanket. The next minute, there was a terrible noise of the animals, and he felt himself being picked up roughly and thrown into a car.

At last, the car stopped and Ponchos was taken out still under the blanket. He seemed to go up some stairs and then into a room, and put onto the floor. The blanket was removed, and Ponchos found himself staring at lots of pairs of eyes in a very dark room.

Trumps and Mr Shorts Jigger looked horrified at this rather dirty factory—made panda. "Is this some sort of a joke?" roared a man who was sitting in a large armchair. "What do you call this halfwit of a creature? Where is my beautiful baby panda?" Ponchos was tired of being insulted by all these Americans and as tired and as frightened as he was, he glared at the man and all the other people in the room.

"I am not a halfwit," he said drawing himself up to his full height. "I am a panda, factory—made in China to the highest standard, and I belong to a very important family from England."

Trumps still had his mouth open as he looked at Ponchos. Mr Shorts

Jigger looked quizzically at him. "I remember you; you were that funny little feller who was on my tour at the Empire State Building. You were making fun of me by jumping up and down. However did you get to be in the panda cage, lying next to a real panda?"

All the men and the women in the room looked at him waiting for an answer. Ponchos thought carefully before responding. "I am doing some work, looking at the life of pandas, and I thought it would be very helpful spending some time at the zoo in the panda house to see how the other half live. I am not impressed as they don't seem to have baths; they eat with their mouths and don't use a knife and fork and as for going to the toilet, on the floor in straw is absolutely disgusting." They all stared in disbelief with their mouths open.

"It was my last day at the panda house before I fly back to England, so if you will excuse me, I need to go and catch my flight." Ponchos made his way to the door.

They all started to laugh and the boss man said, "Oh no, little panda, you are not going anywhere; you will be very useful to us." and with that, he threw Ponchos into a cold, dark and empty room and locked the door.

Chapter 9

Meanwhile back at the zoo, there was pandemonium. The animals were out of their cages for the very first time. They felt a sense of freedom. It all looked so exciting! Sidney and Riley were laughing and running down the road amazed at what they saw. They had no idea what life was like outside of the zoo. There were cars and buses roaring down the highway in every colour you can imagine. People were walking and talking, either to each other or to themselves into little boxes by their ears. Sidney learnt later that these were called mobile phones. Sidney and Riley had forgotten about Ponchos; they were so excited looking at all the new sights and sounds.

Pater Cake walked more slowly feeling rather nervous and not really sure what to do. Pater Cake stared at some people walking by who screamed and ran away looking over their shoulders, crying, "Help, help, call the police." She didn't really understand why people kept screaming when they saw her.

Cars were now coming to a halt and banged into each other as the drivers looked with disbelief what they were seeing. Gorillas, monkeys, elephants all walking down the highway. One driver got out of his car and tried to take a photo of Pater Cake who was furious and never liked having her picture taken. She grabbed the camera and pushed the terrified driver

back in his car. She then promptly sat on the bonnet of the car and pulled the aerial off and threw it in the road. She then made a very rude face, stuck out her tongue and then got of the car, leaving a very large dent where her bottom had been.

Solomon was very angry. Angry with Sidney for messing up the plans, angry with the men who had taken Ponchos. What was he to do now? Hattie gently rubbed his back with her trunk to calm him down.

The animals did not understand the rules of the road, so they wandered in and out the traffic causing absolute chaos. Sirens were sounding and lights were flashing as the police and fire service were coming fast and furiously.

Sidney was having a wonderful time. He had found Wendy's and had helped himself to burgers, buns and milkshakes and was eating them very fast, burping a lot as he was not used to eating so much rich food. His main diet was bananas and fruit. His tummy had begun to feel a bit funny.

Riley was more cautious as he took a few fries out of the bag and put them in his mouth. All the people eating in the restaurant ran out screaming hysterically. They couldn't believe what they were seeing: monkeys, eating burgers and milk shakes! It wasn't possible. Riley and Sidney jumped on the tables and swung on the lampshades, laughing so much their sides hurt.

The police were trying to get the cars to slow down and to stop the panic. The media had arrived, taking videos of the events; this was going to make a great story. One journalist called to the other, "Pandemonium in New

York. That's what we will call the story; haven't had so much fun for years." Bev, who up to now had done very little, promptly grabbed the camera and took pictures of the camera man running very fast down the road straight into Pater Cake who took him in her arms and gave him a very big kiss on the lips. "Now that makes a lovely picture." laughed Bev.

Only Solomon and Hattie realised the seriousness of what was happening. They didn't know what to do so made their way back to the zoo to check on the baby panda.

The police had called all the vets in the area and the zoo keepers to try and get the animals back in the zoo. There was absolute chaos everywhere: the noise of the animals, cars, people screaming, police sirens and fire engines was deafening. No one had ever seen anything like it, an unbelievable sight.

Eventually a cop called Sammy—Jo took control and barked out orders to the keepers and the vets to round up the animals that were having so much fun. The penguins waddling, the monkeys swinging, Bev growling and Pater Cake glaring at anyone who got in the way. My goodness, it was a sight for sore eyes. Eventually, the animals were rounded up and taken back to the zoo by the exhausted keepers and vets. The only sign of the animals having been out of the zoo was the most enormous piles of poo. You had never seen so many types of poo lying in one road; elephant's massive poo, to the small droppings of penguins. What were they going to do with all that poo!

The police were diverting the traffic away from Central Avenue; cars had piled up on top of each other and there were crowds of people all gathering to watch this spectacular scene.

It was only when everything had quietened down and the animals were back in their cages that the head zoo keeper Ben realised that Sidney was missing. Ben couldn't understand what the baby panda was doing in the elephant house all tucked up in a bed of straw fast asleep? He rubbed his head and wondered what on earth had happened. How did the animals get out? Who had let them out? All the cages were unlocked except for the lion enclosure. Where was Trumps, the keeper? No one could find him. What on earth was happening? Ben didn't understand any of it. His head ached.

There was a visit from the President of the United States in a day or two who was coming to view the pandas. What on earth was he going to say; how was he going to explain this? This was going to be the most important day of his career. He was going to entertain the president.

Solomon was very, very worried. No one would look for Ponchos, because no one knew he was missing. Where was Sidney? What was going to happen to him? He feared for his new furry friend and shed a very big tear that ran down his trunk. He didn't know if Ponchos was alive or dead.

Chapter 10

Ponchos was trying very hard not to panic. He was trembling so much his teeth rattled and his bones ached. He had never felt so alone. He lay down and wrapped his arms tightly around his body and tried to sleep. He was just dozing off when he heard a tap at the window and he got up to have a look. He could hardly believe his eyes, there was Sidney grinning at him waving his arms. Ponchos put his paw to his lips to make Sidney be quiet; he was terrified that the men would hear him.

Ponchos whispered through a crack in the window and told Sidney what had happened; how he had been captured by Trumps and Mr Shorts Jigger.

Sidney said, "Don't worry, Ponchos, I know I messed up, but I am going to put it right. I am going to go back and talk to Solomon, he will know what to do."

Sidney jumped of the ledge and called out, "Don't worry, Ponchos, be brave, I'll be back soon."

Sidney never stopped running until he was back at the zoo; he waited until dark then quietly went to see Solomon. Solomon was so startled to see Sidney and relieved that he was safe. Sidney told Solomon what had happened and where Ponchos was being kept prisoner. Solomon woke up Hattie, and they told her the whole story. Hattie shook her enormous head and whispered, "This is very serious; Ponchos is in a very dangerous situation; these people are greedy and will do anything for money. We need to think very carefully about what we should do next."

Sidney sighed and sucked his tail which he always did when he felt bad. He knew he had messed up and if it hadn't been for him, Ponchos would be safe. If only he had done what he was told.

Solomon finally spoke, "We have to lay a trap for the wicked men and women who are in this kidnap gang and have Ponchos. We have to try and expose them for what they are doing. Sidney, you tell Ponchos to tell them that there is going to be an opportunity to kidnap the real baby panda in a few days. The President of the United States is coming to the zoo to see the baby panda the day after tomorrow, just before the pandas are flown back to China."

Hattie spoke quietly, "But Solomon, how is that going to help?" Solomon replied, "Ponchos can pretend to help the gang, but he will lead them right into a trap that we will set up." Sidney looked impressed, "Wow Solomon, what trap would that be?"

"That bit I haven't worked out yet," Solomon sighed.

They all sat still desperately trying to think of a trap that would expose the evil gang and at the same time rescue Ponchos.

"Now let's think this through really carefully. The President is coming

in the afternoon to view the pandas and present an award to the zoo for the best environment for animals. He is bringing some very important people with him including the press from the White House. The visit has been kept a secret. Ben, the head of the zoo, is the only one that knows about the visit, so Trumps will be unaware. Ponchos must convince the gang that he is on their side and will help them to kidnap the panda."

Solomon, Hattie and Sidney put their heads together and came up with a daring plan that would lead the gang into a trap. "Sidney, you need to go and tell Ponchos what we have discussed so far; you need to go over and over the plan with Ponchos until you are sure he understands what he has to do. Sidney, this is your chance to put things right; now don't mess it up."

Chapter 11

Ponchos was feeling a little cheerier since he had spoken to Sidney; at least, someone knew where he was even though that someone was Sidney! Not the most reliable monkey in the world!

Tap, tap, tap at the window caught Ponchos' attention, a bit grin covered his face as he saw Sidney waving his paw. Sidney reported back all that Solomon had said and Ponchos nodded as he tried to take it all in. What great friends he had made, they could have all abandoned him but they hadn't. He was the one who had got them all in this mess and now they were trying to save him. A big tear of gratitude ran down his face as he thanked Sidney and then told him to go before he was noticed.

There was a loud turning of a key and a very mean looking man and woman came in and sat down on the floor.

Ponchos tried a friendly looking smile and got no smile back.

"Right, you pathetic looking bear, start talking." said a very thin and unfriendly looking woman.

Ponchos stuttered, "Look, I was only interested in studying bears and was interested in the baby panda; it wasn't my fault you took the wrong bear. I didn't even like the pandas; they were very rude to me; you can take them for all I care." Ponchos tried to look mean and defiant.

"How do we know you are telling the truth?" the man with the cruel eyes said.

"Why would I care what happens to you? Ponchos replied,

"I'm from England."

The mean looking lady who had a screwed up looking mouth, that reminded Ponchos of a cat's bottom, grabbed him by the arm and threw him roughly onto the floor. "If you want to get out of here in one piece, you better help us get that panda before they leave the zoo; you know the zoo; you have studied the pandas, and you know the layout."

"Yes," said Ponchos, "I do, and I will help you, only you have to do exactly what I tell you, even if it sounds very odd. I know these animals and how it works so you are going to have to trust me."

"Right," said Hilda McSkimming, "I will call a meeting this evening with you and the gang, and you had better have a plan."

"Please, can I have something to eat?" Ponchos asked meekly. "I can't think with an empty tummy." Hilda McSkimming growled and barked at Mr Shorts Jigger to get him some food and off they went.

Ponchos felt very, very nervous; he hoped Sidney would come before the meeting that night, he took some deep breaths, hummed his song and put his thinking hat on.

Mr Shorts Jigger appeared with a pancake that was dry and old. He scowled at Ponchos. "I knew you were trouble, the first time I set eyes on you; I am watching you." Ponchos took the dried—up pancake and ate it because he knew he had to eat something to help him. Mr Shorts Jigger cuffed him round the ear and left.

"Hooray!" thought Ponchos, "A tap at the window, Sidney" An anxious brown face appeared at the window.

"They want me to help them get the baby panda." Ponchos said, "There is a meeting tonight to discuss the plan, I think they trust me."

Ponchos had been given some paper by Hilda McSkimming to write down the instructions, so he used a piece to write down his plan and how the animals would fit into the plan and gave it to Sidney. "Now go, Sidney, and give this to Solomon, don't mess up, this is a very serious business and lives are at stake." Sidney nodded, this time he was determined that he would obey every instruction. But would he get it right?

Chapter 12

Ponchos felt a little calmer as he sat in the chair with all the gang. He knew that he only had one chance to get this right. There was Mr Shorts Jigger and Trumps, who were clearly not the brains of the gang; they looked a bit scared as they knew they had messed up by not being careful with their talking about the kidnap. They had got careless. Ponchos would never had known what was happening if they hadn't discussed the kidnap on the stairs of the Empire State Building.

Clearly, Hilda McSkimming and a man, called The Slasher were in charge. The Slasher had a very large forehead and piercing black eyes, and a look from him made your legs turn to jelly. His eyes were fixed on Ponchos. You didn't mess with a man like that.

"Okay, Panda, talk us through the plan. Don't leave anything out," Hilda McSkimming said.

Ponchos stood up and deliberately did not look at The Slasher and, just for a moment, he forgot he was in rather a dangerous situation. He felt like a commander in the army giving instructions to his troops. He puffed out his chest and then went through the plan slowly and surely until he was confident he had explained everything that needed to be said.

"Well, Panda, you have done well. I think this is a good plan," said

The Slasher. "As you say we leave here at midday, and we will follow the plan and if it is successful, then we will let you become part of our gang and if it isn't, you will be curtains."

Ponchos smiled a fake smile and reminded the gang that however odd the plan might seem, they had agreed that he was in charge, and they would follow it.

Meanwhile back at the zoo, Sidney had delivered the note to Solomon and Hattie, and they both chuckled at Ponchos plan. "Let's hope it works." Hattie sighed, "I've had a bit too much excitement lately, I am looking forward to getting back to normal."

Solomon and Sidney then relayed the plan to all the animals; each one now had learnt to listen and follow the instructions carefully. They understood the risks involved. "Remember, the gang is unaware of the president's visit," said Solomon, "They think Ponchos is part of their gang, and they have no idea that we animals are involved."

For the President's visit an area had been set up just outside of the elephants' enclosure with microphones and speakers so the ceremony could be heard all over the zoo. Tables had been laid out with American-flag table cloths. There were beautiful flowers everywhere and a promise of delicious food. All the keepers would be there, with the president and his very important party of people.

As instructed when no one was looking, Sidney took a

microphone and headed off to the panda house. Sidney of course, had a very important role as he was the only animal who could move about freely as he was still missing.

The keepers were now extra cautious of locking up the animal enclosures after the terrible escape last time.

Sidney briefed Chichi on Ponchos' instructions. She was feeling really guilty because she had been so rude to Ponchos when she first met him, and he had put his whole life at risk to stop the kidnap, so she was very keen to do all that she could to help. The microphone was hidden under some straw in the corner of the house, and Sidney told Chichi when and how to turn it on.

Sidney then ran back to Pater Cake and reminded her of her part in the plan. Pater Cake was based next door to the panda house and because Pater Cake was so enormous, the bars of her enclosure were slightly bigger.

Sidney, Solomon and Hattie went over and over the plan to make sure they hadn't left anything out. Lenny the lion was still feeling very miffed that he hadn't got out on the last adventure, so they were keen to keep him posted.

Chapter 13

The head keeper, Ben, was in a flap. This was the first time that Ben had to prepare for a very important person coming to the zoo. He was very nervous. Life had changed since the animals had got out; they seemed restless and agitated and where was Sidney? Trumps seemed to have disappeared, and he was one of the best keepers at the zoo. He had summoned a meeting for all the keepers at the zoo and had told them about the visit. They were all very excited and had been in early to make sure everything was spotless, and the animals had all been groomed, particularly, the baby panda and his mother.

Everything was in place, and he prayed that it would all go well, and there would be a picture in the newspaper the next day of Ben with the President. He could see the headlines, "Ben, amazing head keeper, wins award for zoo and hosts Chinese Pandas." He smiled at the thought, perhaps he would get a pay rise.

It was nearly time for the President to arrive. Ben put in the finishing touches and then went to the entrance ready to greet the party of important people.

Back with the gang, Ponchos led the way with a gun at the back of his neck. He could feel the hard metal. The Slasher was so close behind him holding the gun and whispering threats in his ear. The Slasher had really smelly breath that wafted into Ponchos' face, making him feel sick. Ponchos was feeling very sick anyway with nerves, and the smelly breath was not helping. Hilda McSkimming, Mr Shorts Jigger and Trumps were following as instructed by Ponchos.

They had come in at a gap in the fence at the exit that Ponchos had remembered seeing when he first visited the zoo. Mr Shorts Jigger was twittering to Trumps and moving his arms and legs in a very uncontrollable way, "I knew this was a bad idea, you see," he hissed, "this panda has been trouble from the moment I set eyes on him."

"Shut up!" Trumps replied, "If it wasn't for your loud voice, the panda wouldn't have heard a thing. It's all your fault, you jitterbug."

"You shut up! How did the animals get out? I bet that was your fault," hissed Mr Shorts Jigger. Both were frightened, The Slasher and Hilda had made it very clear whose fault it was that they had taken the wrong panda. They had been shouted at and threatened with becoming animal food. Hilda had called them idiots and twits and what fools can't tell the difference between a beautiful fluffy new born panda and this scruffy manufactured excuse of a panda.

They were both very keen to shine this time, but they still couldn't work out what went wrong the last time. How did the animals get out? More importantly who had let them out?

Ponchos was walking very carefully; he was holding his breath, terrified that the wrong move would pull the trigger and blow him up in a puff of fur never to see his wonderful family again.

He could hardly breathe, but he kept focused and remembered to stay calm, and take some deep breaths, and keep to the plan. Ponchos, who was normally a bit forgetful, was turning into a brave and adventurous panda. He didn't know he had it in him like so many people but when put to the test, he had surprised himself.

Soon they reached the panda house. Hilda McSkimming and the gang had no idea about the President's visit; they thought it was a typical afternoon at the zoo. They did think it odd that there were not so many people about, which was the case as the zoo had been closed to the public because of the visit for security reasons. The only people who knew were the zoo keepers and their families, and the President and his party.

Hilda McSkimming snapped at Ponchos, "Okay, Panda, what's next? We are at the panda house." Ponchos steadied himself on the gate and said, "Let me go in as planned; you stay here, and I will go and suss out the whereabouts of the baby."

"We have you covered," snarled Hilda McSkimming. "One false move and you are dead, panda fur gloves."

Ponchos scrambled under the gate and walked in to the enclosure; he was partly in sight of Hilda so he had to be very careful. He prayed hard that Sidney had relayed the plan to Solomon, and Solomon had told each animal their part.

He winked at Chichi and whispered very softly, "Don't panic, we are here; in a minute, Hilda and The Slasher will come in, you know what to do."

Chichi looked pale under her black and white face. She trembled, "Ponchos, what happens if it all goes wrong, and they take my baby?" Ponchos whispered, "Chichi, stop it! No time for doubts now; be strong and stay focused. They must not suspect anything; otherwise, we have all had it." The baby stirred, looking anxious, picking up on the tension of his mother and Ponchos, he started to whimper. "Hush, little one." Chichi murmured, "Don't be frightened, I am here."

Ponchos then slipped out and said to Hilda and The Slasher, "Come in now, there is enough room for you to come under the gate on your tummies. Mr Shorts Jigger, you wait by the gorilla's house, stay close to the fence and, Trumps, you wait by the exit by the penguin enclosure. We all now need to get in place, and no one moves until I give a whistle."

Hilda McSkimming and The Slasher slid under the gate, Hilda kicking The Slasher in the face as she kicked her legs through. The Slasher bit his lip to stop from calling out as her high heel poked through his nostril right up his nose. "You, wally burger," he muttered, "you, crazy woman."

Chapter 14

Meanwhile Ben, the head keeper, had greeted the president and his party. Drinks had been provided on arrival and were being handed round by the penguin keepers. The president was a very tall and kind man. He was nearing the end of his term at the White House, and this was one of his last visits as president before he retired. He had been very interested in making sure the animals in zoos were well cared for and had a particular interest in protecting the rarer species from extinction.

Everyone was so excited to meet the president and to get the award. The only person who was feeling very worried was Ben as he still hadn't got over the shame of the animals escaping in his care. It was so important that everything went well today. His very job depended on it.

It was now time for the president to give his speech. The president climbed the platform that had been made especially for him and went to the microphone. The press with their cameras were all in place. Ben held his breath.

Meanwhile back in the Panda enclosure, Hilda McSkimming and The Slasher had finally found their way in and gasped with joy when they saw the baby panda. He was the cutest furry bit of fluff they had ever seen; his big brown eyes looked at them with surprise. Their eyes looked back with greed with the thought of all the money they were going to make from his kidnap.

Outside, Mr Shorts Jigger was getting impatient; he was leaning against the Gorilla enclosure. He was jigging up and down a bit more than usual as he was desperate to do a wee, which always happened when he was nervous.

He was cross. He didn't like being given instructions by Hilda. Before he could take his next breath, he felt a hairy muscly arm wrap around his neck and pull him through the cage. He came face to face with Pater Cake, the gorilla. He groaned loudly; he had been here before. He couldn't move, so great was his fear that he promptly wet himself. Pater Cake stood grinning at him. "Hello, skinflint! I believe we have met before! Fancy being a gorilla with me?" Mr Shorts Jigger had never been so frightened in all his life; he would have screamed except Pater Cake had sat on top of him that had taken all the breath out of his lungs.

Pater Cake was actually a very nice gorilla, but she didn't always know her own strength. "I won't hurt you if you stay very still." she said, which was quite funny as Mr Shorts Jigger couldn't move at all. Pater Cake was pleased she had done what she had been told. All she had to do now was wait.

Trumps meanwhile was by the penguin enclosure as instructed by Ponchos. He was feeling out of control and very angry. "Taking instructions

from a panda, whatever next?" he muttered. Trumps felt something tickling the back of his neck; he turned around, and there was Sidney who unbeknown to him had tied his leg to the fence. He went to move to grab Sidney but promptly fell over. "What the..."

He was furious, but there was nothing he could do. The penguins: Charlie and Gracie, who had been let out by Sidney were waddling up to Trumps. "You traitor," they said, "you are the worst." They cried, "You are a greedy, nasty little man." They stuck a fish in his mouth to keep Trumps quiet.

"Yuk!" said Trumps, "I hate fish; I'm going to be sick."

"Serves you right," the penguins shouted together; and without further ado, they tied him well and truly to the fence with the fish stuck in his mouth. "Why, you look like one of us," they laughed which was true as Trumps was wearing black shorts and a white T-shirt and with his very round tummy, he looked just like a penguin!

The penguins waddled around him in a circle, sticking fish in his shorts, T-shirt and shoes. He smelt terrible!

Trumps could do nothing. He was tied up and with the fish in his mouth, he was unable to shout. He could feel his dream fading away – the wonderful, warm beach, the delicious ice creams! All he could think of now was the strong smell and taste of fish. Yuk!

Chapter 15

Hilda McSkimming and The Slasher were completely unaware of what had happened to Mr Shorts Jigger and Trumps. As far as they knew, the plan was going smoothly, and soon they would have this gorgeous creature in their arms and be away as quickly as possible. They were also unaware that there was a microphone hiding under the straw that Sidney had planted not long ago as part of the plan. Ponchos had carefully made sure that Hilda and The Slasher were both standing in the right position so they would speak clearly into the microphone, not knowing they could be heard all over the zoo.

Ponchos then turned to them and said, "Chichi cannot speak English so they won't know what we are saying. Chichi thinks you are friends of the zoo, having a private viewing of the pandas." Chichi couldn't stop shaking but she knew she had to be very convincing. She smiled at them and gabbled some Chinese Panda noises. Ponchos said to Hilda, "She will let you hold the baby but when she hands the baby to you, smile and talk to her." "What shall I say?" said Hilda.

"Perhaps, you should say what you are really going to do with the panda; she won't understand you."

Chichi slipped her paw under the straw and turned on the

microphone as she had been told. Then she nervously handed the baby to Hilda. The baby began to cry softly at first and then much louder. He didn't like the look of Hilda and The Slasher at all. He tried to wriggle out of Hilda's arms and in doing so kicked her on the nose. He also did a wee that went straight into Hilda's eye!

Hilda grabbed the baby tight, making him cry even louder, she shouted in his face "Why, you smelly, nasty little bear, stop that racket. You are going to make us a lot of money. I am going to make the president pay a lot of money for you if he wants you alive."

Chichi gasped and went even paler. "You are a cruel and heartless old witch and you won't get away with it," Ponchos whispered quietly under his breath.

The Slasher laughed and gave a false sickly smile to Chichi thinking that Chichi didn't understand any of the conversation. "Ha, ha you stupid panda, we are stealing your baby right under your nose. We are going to make a lot of money from your baby."

Ponchos was praying that his plan was all working. He prayed that Mr Shorts Jigger was in the Gorilla cage safely tucked underneath Pater Cake.

Trumps was with the penguins tied up and unable to shout for help. He hoped the microphone was working and the president who was about to give his speech could hear what was being shouted in the panda house and realise that there was about to be a kidnap and come running to help them.

He trembled, what if it all goes wrong? The baby panda will be kidnapped. Ponchos most certainly would be killed off and made into gloves, and he would never see his lovely family ever again. A big tear rolled down his cheek. He then pulled himself together. He had to stay focused and believe that all would be well.

He immediately turned his attention to The Slasher and Hilda and said in a very loud voice into the hidden microphone. "Hilda McSkimming and The Slasher. You are both very wicked people. Your plan to kidnap the baby panda to make money and to embarrass the President of the United States will not work. Evil never wins if good men, women and animals do something to stop it. Even if they are ordinary, not particularly brave and are very frightened. Today, this ends and having you behind bars will make all the animals in the zoos a safer place."

Hilda and The Slasher looked very astonished. "Nice speech, panda. You don't frighten us." They grabbed Ponchos and the baby panda and ran out of the panda house running as fast as they could.

Chapter 16

The president looked at Ben who was now smiling, "Phew" he breathed a sigh of relief, all was going to plan. As the President opened his mouth a sound of crying was heard over the microphone, first softly and then getting louder. The president shut his mouth in astonishment and looked around to see where the crying was coming from. Then the sound of different voices could be heard from one of the speakers loud and clear. The voices were coming from a man and woman talking about the kidnapping of a baby panda and people making a lot of money and then a very loud voice boomed over the speaker talking about good overcoming evil and people behind bars.

What on earth was happening! The president looked puzzled and Ben looked as though he was about to faint! In fact, he did right there on the president's feet. Crash, band wallop!

The President who was used to taking control shouted to his security men, "Run to the panda house, I think a kidnap is taking place." At that moment, Sidney rushed forward and grabbed the president's hand pulling him towards the panda house. The men and women following closely behind.

They arrived just in time to see Hilda McSkimming running out of the panda house with the baby in her arms with The Slasher close behind, dragging Ponchos by the ear. Ponchos bit The Slasher on his leg, making him scream with pain. Ponchos took his chance and tripped him up, The Slasher fell flat on his face right into a pile of animal poo. Ponchos grabbed the baby panda from Hilda just in time as she tripped over The Slasher and did a somersault high in the air, landing smack on The Slasher's head. A furious and spitting Hilda tried to kick the president in the leg with her high heeled shoes as he held her down. "Ouch!" The President cried as the heel dug into his calf, "You, nasty thief, you will pay for what you have done."

Meanwhile the security men and women had caught up breathless from running, put handcuffs on Hilda and The Slasher's wrists. They were well and truly caught! "Idiot!" cried The Slasher to Hilda, "I told you, we couldn't trust that panda, now look what you have done, you've ruined everything."

"What panda are you talking about?" said the president.

"The scruffy manufactured one from China, of course," said Hilda. "The one who spoilt all our plans; the one who must be working for you."

In all the excitement, the President hadn't noticed Ponchos. He looked with surprise at a very dirty and scruffy creature crept out of The Slasher's legs. Ponchos suddenly felt very shy. He had never met a president before. He didn't know how to behave. "Hello, Mr President," he stuttered, "My name is Ponchos. I am from England. It's a very long story. I lost my family because I was nosy. I heard men talking about kidnapping a baby panda and making a lot of money." Ponchos couldn't say anymore. He was so tired.

The President looked gobsmacked. Before he could say another word, there was a loud sound of grunting and shouting. They all walked towards the awful noise. They all burst out laughing when they saw Trumps with a bright red face and bulging eyes. He had a fish in his mouth and three very pleased looking penguins sitting on his tummy. They laughed even louder when they spotted a very happy looking Pater Cake sitting on a thin man with wispy hair, hissing.

The president had never been so surprised in his life. He had come across many different situations in his time as president, but never one like this.

He turned to Ponchos and said, "You and the animals are all heroes; you have done something amazing. I want to hear the whole story."

"Mr President," the men from the newspaper shouted, "We have got the whole story live on camera; please can we have an interview with you and this little panda. This is going to make the best story ever it all yet. We have recorded this on the television all over the world. Everyone will know how brave Ponchos and the animals have been."

Chapter 17

Ben, the keeper, had come too after fainting with shock on the president's feet and thought he must be in the middle of some very peculiar and frightening dream all about a panda and a president. Then he realised this was not a dream but was actually happening. He was just wondering how he was going to explain everything to his boss when he was being patted on the back and congratulated for having the best animals in the world and the best story about the zoo which would bring in millions of dollars.

He was about to open his mouth and then closed it quickly as his boss came forward and shook his hand. "Ben, you are going to have a big promotion; you have made this zoo famous, and we will get a lot of money as a result of this story. I am going to make you the Director of the zoo." Ben could hardly speak; could this really be true? He looked around at the animals; it was almost like they were smiling but, of course, that was impossible. He muttered his thanks and gingerly sat down trying to take it all that had happened. What an extraordinary day it had been.

Ponchos could hardly believe his eyes! Here he was sitting next to one of the most powerful men in the whole world, the President of the United States and he was listening to him, a mere panda, a scruffy one at that!

The president asked Ponchos if he could give an interview on the television. He could see that Ponchos was very tired but felt they all needed to hear the whole amazing story.

So, this brave and very kind panda with the microphone under his nose and the cameras all rolling began his story starting from the very beginning. He didn't want to leave anything out. The falling out of the rucksack. Being lost and alone on the stairs of the Empire State Building.

How he called the fire brigade to get out of the building (he was a bit worried that he would get a telling off for wasting the fire services time).

His trip to Wendy's and how he stole a burger and milkshake (oops, another naughty bit).

The trip to the zoo and overhearing Trumps and Mr Shorts Jigger wanting to steal the baby panda to make money. He talked about meeting Solomon and how all the animals had been involved to stop the kidnap. Then how it all went wrong. (Ponchos didn't mention Sidney's big mistake as he didn't want to make him look bad.)

How he had come to be kidnapped instead of the baby panda. How frightened he was when he was taken to the gang and met with The Slasher and Hilda McSkimming.

How he was thrown in a dark room and cried at the thought of never seeing his beloved family again. A big tear rolled down his face as he longed for Rebekah, Anna, Eliza and Hettie.

He went onto say how Sidney had found him. The plan that Solomon,

Hattie and Ponchos had hatched to lead the crooks into a trap. He said how he knew about the president's visit and how a microphone system would be set up in the panda enclosure. The Slasher and Hilda's plan would be heard by the president. He talked about the plan to stop Trumps and Mr Shorts Jigger by Pater Cake and the marvellous Penguins. Ponchos gave a little laugh at this point!

At last he finished, and there was a sound of silence. Then the loudest roar of praise and clapping. Everyone stood up clapping and clapping.

After all the noise had died down, the president stood up and said, "Ponchos, you are one of the bravest and kindest (the president stopped), err, person, animal? and hero of the United States of America. You just ask for anything you want, and you will have it."

Chapter 18

Back in England in a little village in Oxfordshire a family were watching a programme on wildlife together. Rebekah, Anna, Eliza and Hettie loved programmes about wildlife, and this particular programme was all about elephants in India. They were enjoying the programme when suddenly a news flash came across the screen. "Breaking news, we go live to New York. Unbelievable story! Panda saves the day."

"I wonder what all this is about?" Anna said, "It makes me feel sad because we lost our lovely Ponchos in New York and as hard as we tried, we could not find him."

"Yes," said Eliza, "Mum even wrote to the Empire State Building when we came home, to see if we had lost him there."

"I know," Hettie said with tears in her eyes, "We hoped so much someone would find him." The girls sat there remembering their great friend and how much they had missed him.

Ponchos had been so missed by Rebekah and her sisters. There wasn't one day that they hadn't thought about him. They were so worried that he was lost and alone in a very big city. How would he manage? Who would look after him?

Rebekah said sadly, "The trouble is Ponchos isn't a very clever

panda; he is a bit nervous and forgetful; he will never find his way home."
They all looked very sad and worried.

"Bother," said Hettie, "what is this news flash?"

Rebekah went to turn the television off and just as she was about to do so, Anna called out, "Wait, I think I saw Ponchos."

Eliza and Hettie laughed, "Saw Ponchos, Anna? I don't think so." Then they all went very quiet.

There suddenly on the screen in full view was Ponchos, there was no doubt it was him. He looked scruffy as usual, dirtier and a bit thinner. He stood in that way he always did when he was nervous on one leg scratching his left ear. What on earth had Ponchos got to do with a news flash about New York?

The girls called their parents, and they all sat down absolutely gobsmacked as they heard Ponchos describe his adventures since they lost him in the Empire State Building. They leapt up in excitement. "Ponchos, Ponchos!" they shouted at the television, "You are a hero. You are a star, but best of all, you are alive."

At the end of the interview, they heard the president say to Ponchos that he was awarded the very highest honour of the United States of America and he could ask for anything, anything at all and he would get it.

There was a pause as everyone leant forward, including the family in Oxfordshire as they heard Ponchos whisper very quietly,

"I want to go home."

The president gently put his hand on Ponchos arm. "Of course, you can go home, Ponchos, just tell me where your home is."

The family held their breath. Would Ponchos remember his address?

Ponchos smiled and then repeated very clearly his address,

"Blackberry House,

Habitat Way,

Gatehill,

Oxfordshire,

England."

The President then asked for a phone and there and then rang the phone number of the family in Oxfordshire. He invited them all over to America to be his personal guests at the White House. They would watch Ponchos being given the highest award in America.

Ponchos was taken by the president to stay in the White House. He was so tired he could hardly keep awake.

Mrs President ran him a hot, soapy bath with lots of bubbles and then carefully dried him with a soft enormous towel. He then put on the President's dressing gown and sat down to a delicious supper of pancakes and blueberries. He was so full he could hardly move and as the President was talking to him, he felt his eyes close and his head drop onto the table gently snoring.

The President helped him get into the biggest bed he had ever seen and then he slept soundly dreaming of meeting his family in the morning.

Chapter 19

You would have had to have been there to see the excitement and joy as Ponchos met his family. There were tears and laughter, joy and sorrow, shouting and silence as they were all together again. They hugged and kissed and held onto Ponchos, never wanting to let him go.

Ponchos asked the president if he could take his family to the zoo and meet his friends. He wanted to thank them for all that they had done to help him. The president said he wanted to come as well to thank them and give them medals.

Whilst the President was talking to Ben, the head keeper, Ponchos quietly slipped away with the girls. They first went to Solomon and Hattie. Ponchos threw his arms around their trunks and kissed them. The wisest friends he had ever met. He would never forget them. They were the first to get their medals and the president spent a lot of time talking to them.

Ponchos took the girls to meet Sidney and Riley. Ponchos took Sidney aside and kissed him. Sidney was still a bit worried that Ponchos was still cross with him for messing things up. Ponchos took his arm and said, "Sidney, we all get things wrong and make mistakes. All is forgiven, and now we are the best of friends." Sidney and Riley jumped up onto the platform to get their medals. They were so happy; they had never had a medal before.

Rebekah, Anna, Eliza and Hettie loved the penguins. They looked so funny waddling up to the president to receive their awards. They looked so smart in their black and white coats.

Ponchos took the girls to meet Pater Cake who gave them rides on her back as she made her way up to the platform to receive her medal. The President looked a little alarmed as this great big gorilla climbed up onto the platform.

Finally, Ponchos went to the panda enclosure and spoke to Chichi. Chichi said she would never ever forget Ponchos and would always have him in her heart.

Ponchos whispered in Chichi's ear. "By the way Chichi, what is the name of the baby panda?"

Chichi whispered very quietly back into Ponchos ear and said, "His name is Otto Theodore."

Rebekah, Anna, Eliza and Hettie suddenly spotted the baby panda. They, like Ponchos, fell in love with him straight away. "He is so cute." Eliza said, "Can we keep him?" Chichi and Ponchos gave a very loud "NO" and then fell about laughing together.

Ponchos decided to wave to Lenny who was still muttering to himself about being left out of the fun. Anna and Eliza stood a little way back, a bit nervous of this growling lion but grateful for his part in rescuing the panda.

At last, it was time for Ponchos to receive his award. There were so many people and animals clapping and cheering as they watched this brave and kind panda climb up onto the stage to meet the president and receive his medal.

And this is where I leave you, dear reader, with a very happy family back with their precious friend. A friend that was lost to them but now found. I am sure they will never let him out of their sight again, or will they?